"A wonderful, sensitive story about children's feelings of sadness and loss after the death of a loved one…"

—*School Library Journal*

"The rich colors and many details in the artwork give the pictures great warmth, and London's simple, heartfelt handling of a child's grief experience is right on target for the age group."

—*Booklist*

"London's impressively visual narrative…is given even greater dimension by Long's exquisitely detailed art. Words and pictures create an affecting work that will be especially meaningful to children who have lost a loved one."

—*Publishers Weekly*

"Jonathan London's tender story of understanding, comfort, and hope is enhanced by Sylvia Long's richly detailed drawings… a delight for the ears and the eyes."

—*The Five Owls*

To the memory of
Grandma Sittenreich and Nana London, and for Peggy Dunn,
a teacher whose life is love.   — J.L.

To my grandmothers,
Sylvia Nichols Lyman and Margaret Mitchell Carlisle,
whose stars shine brightly still.   — S.L.

ISBN 0-590-51913-1

Text copyright © 1994 by Jonathan London. Illustrations copyright © 1994 by Sylvia Long.
All rights reserved. Published by Scholastic Inc., 555 Broadway, New York, NY 10012, by arrangement with Chronicle Books. SCHOLASTIC and associated logos are trademarks and/or registered trademarks of Scholastic Inc.

12 11 10 9 8 7 6 5 4 3 2 1   8 9/9 0 1 2 3/0

Printed in the U.S.A.   14

First Scholastic printing, September 1998

Book design by Laura Jane Coats. Typeset in Stempel Garamond and Charlemagne.

LIPLAP'S WISH

written by
Jonathan London

illustrated by
Sylvia Long

SCHOLASTIC INC.
New York Toronto London Auckland Sydney

One winter morning, Liplap woke up and looked out his window. The first snowfall had covered his yard with a blanket of sparkling white!

He quickly tugged on his winter clothes
and hopped outside — *lip-lap, lip-lap* —
and got right down to work, rolling
and shaping the snow. Soon he had made
a snowbunny. But it didn't have a face.

"I wish," thought Liplap, "Grandma
could see my snowbunny. She'd know
how to make it look really great.
She'd know how to give it a face."

But Grandma hadn't lived to see
the snow this year. Liplap still couldn't
believe it. He kept expecting to see
her step from his house.

Liplap hopped back inside — *lip-lap, lip-lap* —
and rummaged in the old satin-lined box
where Grandma kept ribbons and bobbins
and knickknacks and things.

Then he hopped back outside
and poked in five different kinds of
buttons for the snowbunny's coat.
He still half hoped Grandma would
come out to see his snowbunny.

The front door opened.
His father waved and said, "Liplap!
Your snowbunny has no face!"

Suddenly, Liplap felt like crying.
He hopped right by his father
and back into bed.

Liplap's mother brought him carrot cake
and hot cocoa, still steaming,
but Liplap didn't feel like eating.
She patted his back, and sang him a lullaby
until he drifted off to sleep.

Later that day, Liplap once again looked
out his window. The setting sun was pulling
rose and yellow scarves across the sky.
His snowbunny looked cold.

Liplap quickly bundled up again and hopped
outside — *lip-lap*, *lip-lap*. He threw his own scarf
around the snowbunny's shoulders, his rumpled
cap on the snowbunny's head.

Liplap pulled off his mittens and slid them over the snowbunny's snow paws. He cupped his own cold little paws and blew on them the way Grandma used to do.

Liplap shivered. He peered hard at the snowbunny's face, then he dug down into the moist earth and found three shiny pebbles.

With the black stones he made two shiny eyes and a little black nose. Then with some pine needles he made the snowbunny's whiskers.

The snowbunny's eyes gleamed tiny lights from the last of the sun…then went dark. Something went dark inside of Liplap, too. He found a stick and carved a frown in the snowbunny's face. Then he hopped back into his house feeling very sad.

That night, Liplap's mother knelt
with him at the bedroom window.

"There's an old Rabbit's tale," she said,
"that your grandma used to tell. It's about
how, long ago, when the First Rabbits died,
they became stars in the sky. And to this day,
they come out at night and watch over us.
And they remind us that our loved ones
shine forever in our hearts. That's why
we wish upon a star."

"Do you think Grandma
    is a star?" asked Liplap.

"Well, look there," said
    his mother, pointing to
    the sky. "See that low star
    shining white — as white
    as Grandma's fur?"

"Do you think that's her?"
    asked Liplap eagerly.

"I think you could wish it
    were," answered his mother.
    Liplap closed his eyes
    and wished.

    And when he opened his eyes,
    that white star seemed to wink
    and sparkle. It made him tingle.

"Now she's with us forever,"
    he said, as he curled up in bed.
    Soon Liplap was dreaming.

The next morning, when Liplap
hopped outside — *lip-lap, lip-lap* —
he saw that the frown on the
snowbunny's face had melted.
In its place, Liplap stuck a carrot.

"Are you hungry, Snowbunny?"
he asked. "*I* am."

Then Liplap ate *five* carrots —
one for each point of a star.

Jonathan London lives in Northern California with his wife and two sons. He has written many books for children including *If I Had A Horse, The Eyes of Gray Wolf, Honey Paw and Lightfoot, Condor's Egg* and *Hip Cat* also published by Chronicle Books.

Sylvia Long is the illustrator of several books for children including the bestselling *Hush Little Baby* and *Ten Little Rabbits.* Ms. Long lives in Arizona with her husband and their two sons, Matthew and John.